# Sea Treasure

Story by Rose Inserra
Illustrations by Lisa Manuzak Wiley

## Contents

## Chapter 1

# Welcome to Silver Cove

*These school holidays are beginning to feel like a disaster*, thought Charlie.

Charlie and his twin sister, Belle, and their parents, Dad and James, were going to a seaside town for a week. The narrow road they had been driving along for over three hours wound dangerously in places.

They got a glimpse of the ocean, but the beach looked far away, and the road was steep. On top of that, the weather was terrible – it was windy and rainy.

"I can't see much out of my window," said Charlie.

"Look!" cried Belle. She was pointing ahead. "I can just make out the lighthouse! We must be almost there."

Welcome to Silver Cove
Welcome to
SILVER
COVE

Dad drove past a road sign that said "Welcome to Silver Cove". Right after, they found the entrance to their holiday cabins.

Belle raced out of the car towards their cabin, which was called "Treasure Trove Cabin". She didn't mind getting wet in the rain.

Charlie *did* mind getting wet. He put on his raincoat and hood and shivered next to Belle as they waited for Dad and James to unlock the door.

"I wonder why our cabin is called 'Treasure Trove'," said Belle.

Charlie shrugged his shoulders. "I don't know. And it looks like the cabin next door is called 'Shipwreck Treasure'," he replied.

SHIPWRECK
TREASURE CABIN
TREASURE TROVE
CABIN

It rained heavily all night, and in the morning, it had turned into a drizzle. Charlie had been hoping for fun times in the sunshine, but it looked as if it was going to be spoilt by the rain and the cold.

They waited a while for the drizzle to clear, but it looked to have set in for the morning. Charlie wouldn't be needing his sun hat or sunscreen. He put on his jacket and pulled up his hood instead.

"This holiday is a disaster!" said Charlie. "With this weather, there'll be no swimming or building sandcastles, and no bodysurfing or fishing! I wish I was back home!"

"I know it's not good weather, Charlie, but I'm sure it will clear soon. Then we can go to the beach," said Dad. "Anna at the reception desk said there are caves on the beach where looters who stole treasure from shipwrecks used to hide out."

"I've found some things we can do in the wet weather," said James, holding out his phone. "We have tickets for the Shipwreck Museum and a tour of the Silver Cove Lighthouse."

Charlie and Belle looked at one another, feeling disappointed. They weren't sure they would see anything like looters' treasure at the museum or the lighthouse.

*At least it will be dry and warm*, Charlie thought as they walked to the car, with Belle jumping over puddles.

## Chapter 2

# A Visit to the Museum

Dave, the guide at the Shipwreck Museum, invited them to come in and have a look around. Belle and Charlie walked past displays of old objects from shipwrecks. There were hundreds of items. The signs said that some were over two hundred years old.

Dave explained that when ships crashed against the rocks, they were damaged and they sank. The ships carried cargo such as wool, steel, timber, food, equipment, furniture, gold and silver coins, as well as people's belongings. When a ship was wrecked, these objects floated to shore.

In the displays, there were buttons from clothing, a watch, a ship's bell, drinking glasses, dinner plates, cutlery, bowls, furniture and fittings, tools, utensils, clothing, ceramic pots and jars, glass bottles, wooden objects, leather and rope.

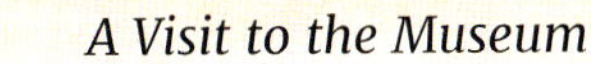

"We think there are about three million shipwrecks on the ocean floor all over the world that have not been found yet," Dave explained.

He continued. "They are very hard to find in the deep ocean because the sand covers them up over many years. And when they are found, it's dangerous to raise them out of the water because they can break up after being submerged for so long."

"Do coins break up, too?" asked Charlie.

"The gold coins remain in better condition than coins made from silver and other metals," Dave replied. "The salt in the ocean corrodes those types of coins, which means the salt water wears them down."

"I hope we find gold ones when we go to the beach," said Belle.

"Nobody is allowed to keep an object that may be from a wreckage," Dave said. "It's called looting if you do."

"Are there any shipwrecks that have been found around here lately?" Charlie asked.

"As a matter of fact, yes. A shipwreck has just been discovered not far offshore from here. We think it's the *Alexander* – a ship that sank about one hundred and fifty years ago," said Dave.

"James! Dad! Can we please go to the beach now? We want to look for some treasure," Belle pleaded.

"Not now. It's still raining. And we've already booked the lighthouse tour," said James.

They all decided that after the lighthouse tour, they would go to the beach for a treasure hunt. Maybe the weather would be fine by then.

Chapter 3

# The Lighthouse Tour

The lighthouse stood tall on a hill near the water's edge. It was white with a red roof.

"Hi, my name is Josie. Welcome to the Silver Cove Lighthouse. I'll show you around," said the lighthouse guide.

The lighthouse tour was more interesting than Belle and Charlie had thought it would be. They all climbed up the spiral staircase inside the lighthouse. It took a while to climb all one hundred and thirty-five steps, but the view from the top was worth the effort.

"Oh, wow! I can see so far away. Is that a whale?" asked Belle.

"It could be. They come this way during this time of year," said Josie.

"Why are there so many shipwrecks at Silver Cove?" asked Charlie.

"The ocean is very rough here. The weather can change quickly. In the olden days, the ships were dragged along in the heavy seas. By the time ships' captains saw these high cliffs, it was too late. They would crash on the rocks, and then against the cliffs," Josie explained.

"Is that why they put a lighthouse here?" asked Belle.

"Yes, the light from the lighthouse warned the ships that they were close to shore. There were fewer accidents after they built the lighthouse," Josie said.

"Dave from the Shipwreck Museum said there was a new wreck that was found close to here," said Charlie.

"Yes, that's right. We're not sure yet, but we think it could be the *Alexander*. There are divers all the way over there now," said Josie, and she pointed to a boat in the distance.

Charlie looked through a set of binoculars. He could see the boat and two divers in wetsuits. He imagined the treasures they might find in the shipwreck, and wished he could be a shipwreck diver, too.

When the tour was finished, Charlie, Belle, Dad and James went back down the stairs. As they stepped outside, they heard a rumble of thunder. There were dark clouds in the sky, promising more rain.

"I guess we won't be going to the beach now," said Charlie in a sad voice.

Belle and Charlie were disappointed. They had been looking forward to beachcombing and finding some lost treasures from the *Alexander*.

"There's always tomorrow," said Dad.

Chapter 4

# Beachcombing

It rained all night, but by morning the skies had cleared, and the sun was poking through the clouds.

Finally, after breakfast, Charlie, Belle, Dad and James went to the beach. Charlie was in a hurry to look at the debris scattered over the sand. He was hoping there were coins that might have washed up from the *Alexander*.

They spent two hours looking for anything that might be treasure. But all they found was old fishing line, seaweed, driftwood and some rubbish that lined the shore after last night's storm.

For lunch, they took a break from the treasure hunt and ate their sandwiches under a beach umbrella. It was warm, now. The sun was shining brightly, and people were beginning to gather on the beach.

Belle and Charlie watched the seagulls circling them for food, ready to feed on scraps.

"Dad, can we go and have one more look for treasure?" asked Charlie.

"Okay, but just one more look," said Dad.

Belle had her sand bucket ready. They were both hoping they would find something this time.

It only took a few minutes for Belle to find some pieces of sea glass and put them in her bucket. Charlie had no luck finding anything that remotely looked like shipwreck treasure. His most interesting find was a hermit crab.

Just as they were about to walk back to the beach umbrella, Charlie's toe touched something hard. He bent down to pick it up. Part of it was round like a coin, and it didn't look like it had been corroded by the salty water. Maybe it was valuable! He would take it to the museum tomorrow and see if there was anything like it on display.

For now, it was time to go back to the cabin.

Chapter 5

# The Night Market

Belle and Charlie were tired after all the beachcombing.

"Let's have an early night," said James. "We'll go out again in the morning."

As Belle and Charlie were resting, voices and laughter could be heard coming from the beach through the open window of their cabin.

There was a knock on their door. It was Anna from the reception desk.

"Everyone is at the beach. There's a night market on tonight. Come and join us," she said.

Belle and Charlie were very excited. They were no longer tired, and they were feeling a little bit hungry. They couldn't wait to have some of the delicious night market food.

Charlie grabbed his treasure. Maybe Dave from the museum or Josie from the lighthouse would be there, too, and he could ask them if his treasure really *was* a valuable coin.

The beach was filled with people, young and old. Bright fairy lights lit up the stalls that lined the shore.

The night sky blazed with stars. Music and the aroma of delicious food filled the beach. People sat on the sand talking to each other, laughing and taking photos.

Charlie and Belle were eating ice cream when Charlie saw a familiar face in the distance.

"Oh, look! There's Josie," cried Charlie.

Josie was just arriving at the market when Charlie ran up to her excitedly.

"I found something on the beach today. I think it's an old coin, and it's not too worn away … I mean, corroded," said Charlie, holding out his treasure.

Josie shone her flashlight and had a close look.

"It could be a coin or a gold button someone lost on the beach, Charlie. Or it could be something washed up from the *Alexander*. Sometimes things can float ashore," said Josie.

"Maybe I should show it to Dave at the Shipwreck Museum," said Charlie.

"That's a great idea," said Josie. "He knows more about shipwreck treasure than I do!"

Chapter 6

# A Special Find

"So, it's not a coin?" Charlie asked Dave at the museum the next morning.

"No, Charlie, it's better than a coin," said Dave. "It's a gold ring that's been made from a coin. It's very special. And I think I know where it came from."

Dave took out an old photo of a ship's captain in uniform. There, on the captain's hand, was the exact same ring!

Charlie learned that the ring belonged to Captain Leroy, whose ship, the *Alexander*, was wrecked off the coast around one hundred and fifty years ago – the same wreck that the divers were working on!

"It's a great find, Charlie. We now know for sure the wreck is the *Alexander*," said Dave. "The ring must have dropped out of the captain's treasure chest when the divers moved it, and then floated to shore. You are lucky to have found it."

Dave explained how the ring was special because the coin was very valuable. It was made out of pure gold.

"We'd love to display the ring here in a special cabinet, along with any other treasure the divers find on the wreck," said Dave.

"Can we come back and see it any time?" asked Belle.

"Of course," replied Dave. "We will write up the story about how Charlie found it, and put it in our brochure and on our website."

It was raining again, but Charlie was no longer annoyed. He put on his jacket and walked outside. He was very proud and excited that he had found an important treasure.

"It's lucky we had the bad weather, or we wouldn't have known anything about these valuable objects from shipwrecks," said James.

"Where shall we go for our next holiday?" asked Dad. "Somewhere warmer?"

"Let's come back to Silver Cove!" Charlie cried out.

"Yes! It has to be Silver Cove. Now it's *my* turn to find some sea treasure!" said Belle.